BIBLE POSITIONS ON POLITICAL ISSUES

BIBLE POSITIONS ON POLITICAL ISSUES

BY JOHN C. HAGEE
WITH SANDY HAGEE PARKER

First Printing August 2004

ISBN# 1-59608-12-7

Contents

CHAPTER 1, PAGE 1

Let Your Voice Be Heard

CHAPTER 2, PAGE 25

The Family God Intended

CHAPTER 3, PAGE 49

Defending the Defenseless

CHAPTER 4, PAGE 73

Attack on Christianity

CHAPTER 5, PAGE 91

Making an Impact

1

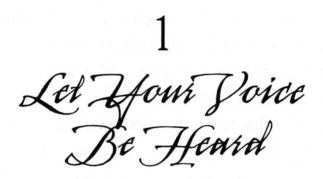

"Our laws and our institutions must
necessarily be based upon the teachings of
the Redeemer of Mankind. It is impossible
that it should be otherwise; and in this sense
and to this extent, our civilization and our
institutions are emphatically Christian."

—U.S. Supreme Court
1892

Those words, uttered by our nation's highest court a
little over one hundred years ago, show that the
Supreme Court once held the Word of God in the center

of our country's moral and political compass. Now, however, as the gavel falls in that same court, it does not hold that same Book in the esteem it once did. First the Court turned its back on the Bible; now it turns its back on the United States Constitution. What lies ahead? Scripture has an answer for everything, but what most may not know is that the Bible even has clear and distinct positions on political issues. If we are to live our lives by the Word of God and obey all of His commands, then we must be acutely aware of what is said in that Word regarding the world today. Matthew 5:16 tells us to "let our light shine before men." This New Testament principle presents a profound truth that should be the clarion call for all Christians in America today—to let your light shine. Don't curse the darkness; let your light shine now!

What exactly is meant by such a mandate? Simply this: it's our duty, as Christians, to let the light of the gospel shine in our lives with the power and force that God intended. In an American Religious Identification Survey, over 76.5 percent of the American adult population claim to be Christian; if this is the truth, why are we not a dominant force in politics and shaping our country's moral fabric?[1] It does not require profound

---

[1] Professor Barry A. Kosmin et al. "American Religious Identification Survey," Graduate Center at the City University of New York 2000 *(www.gc.cuny.edu)*

intellectual insights to understand that our nation is headed down a pathway of moral and spiritual destruction. In the meantime, the church hides the light of God from a world that so desperately needs to be illuminated. Instead of allowing our light to shine through our lives, we sit idly by and curse the darkness we have allowed to perpetuate. When this is the case, the church is not a dynamic force of change; rather it's a mere reflection of the decaying culture around us.

We can change our rotting society and restore it to what God intended. We, the people, in these United States have the responsibility to change anything in our society that destroys the moral foundations on which our nation was founded. Our first objective is to change ourselves and let our light shine as the "city on a hill that cannot be hidden."[2]

Jesus did not hesitate to call leaders of His day hypocrites—literally, "mask wearers." He was against their showy, superficial, and abhorrent religious pretense. They tried to present a public image completely different from whom and what they really were. As Christians, we have no right to demand things from our leaders or fellow brothers and sisters in Christ

---

[2] Matthew 5:14

that we do not demand from ourselves. By putting on a false sense of spirituality we are not fooling God or those around us; we are only turning people away from God. The following are some examples of how Christians can allow these attitudes to rob them of their light. We will focus on Biblical positions on political issues in the following chapters.

"Suppose a Nation in some distant region should take the Bible for their only Law Book, and every member should regulate his conduct by the precepts there exhibited...What a paradise would this region be!"

—John Adams
1756 America's Second President

First of all, you say that you are against abortion, but what do you do to aid young girls in trouble? What does your church do? Do you provide counseling and hope for the future? Do you offer food, medical, and financial support? Or do you merely cavil against teen pregnancies and judge those who are in such a predicament? When the church offers no alternative, where else are these girls supposed to go but to the world? What are you doing to make a realistic difference in the lives of hurting people facing difficult choices in their own personal abortion debate?

Regarding the issue of homosexuality, the Bible is crystal clear that this act is an abomination to the Lord. In Leviticus 20 the Lord discusses punishments for sin with Moses. Verse 13 records the Lord's view of homosexuality: "If a man lies with a man as one lies with a woman, both of them have done what is detestable." Yet why do we act as though homosexuality or lesbianism is worse that cheating, stealing, being a murderer or a hypocrite?

AIDS patients are dying painful, impoverished, isolated deaths because they chose a homosexual lifestyle; yet Christians by and large have not figured out that compassion toward sinners, in their time of need, does not equate to condoning their sin. Jesus is tough on sin, but tender toward the sinner. He died for all of us.

Welfare reform has been a major voting issue ever since LBJ's Great Society. Put very simply, this "reform" is nothing more than taking money from a man who *will* work and giving it to a man who *will not*. Since that time, over five trillion dollars in government aid has been paid out to remove poverty from our society. Despite this, the percentage of those with incomes under the poverty level has been greater since liberal government activists started taking money from the pocketbooks of those who were working and giving it to those who refused employment.

The welfare program in this country has shattered the family structure of those in the lower income brackets and has virtually guaranteed generational dependence on the dole. Today millions of Americans are dependent upon welfare.[3] Although the welfare program has amounted to nothing more than a moral and economic morass, the Church cannot close its eyes to the truly needy who reside in our midst. While working citizens should not be obligated to finance the lifestyles of those who can work but won't—one cannot assume that everybody in dire economic situations falls in that category.

In the New Testament, Paul laid out a rule stating, "If a man will not work, he shall not eat."[4] Similarly, James wrote, "Suppose a brother or sister is without clothes and daily food. If one of you says to him, 'Go, I wish you well; keep warm and well fed,' but does nothing about his physical needs, what good is it?"[5] When we debate issues like welfare reform, abortion, or homosexual

---

3 U.S. Department of Health and Human Services: *Administration for Children and Families*—Statistical Data, March 2004
4 I Thessalonians 3:10

rights, we must remember that those who lack money, have immoral lifestyles, or find themselves pregnant out of wedlock, are not our enemies. Our battles are not with flesh and blood— we are fighting a spiritual war.

"It is the duty of all nations to acknowledge the Providence of Almighty God, to obey His will, to be grateful for His benefits, and to humbly implore His protection and favor."

— George Washington

October 3, 1789
Proclaiming a National Day of Prayer and Thanksgiving.

We have no right to complain about something we have the ability to change. The gospel holds the transforming power of change. In a teaching by John Maxwell he stated, "The problem with the church today is that they don't want miracles, they want magic." He makes a very real observation: while Christians complain about wanting to change our government—hoping that abortion will become illegal and crossing their fingers, eager to see homosexual marriage banned—we actually do nothing to see those dreams become reality. We must not discount the supernatural power of God for one moment; the miracle-working power of God has

---

5 James 2:15-16

never ceased. We need to let His supernatural power flow from the Church into our world. "If God be for us, who can be against us?"[6]

Those who prefer to feel inadequate and choose to believe that one person cannot change anything are truly mistaken. Numerous times throughout history the power of one person has changed the masses. Biblically speaking, Esther, just one woman, saved the Jewish people from annihilation. A more modern example is Rosa Parks; her one action, refusing to move to the back of a bus, ignited the civil rights movement and changed our nation forever.

The motivation of one person can indeed change the face of the world. For instance, British statesman Wilberforce dedicated his entire career to ending slavery in Britain in the 1800's. His passion drove him to create a unity among politicians from all parties who endeavored to free the oppressed in their nation.[7] Although Wilberforce and his union were threatened with violence and malignant press and their lives and careers placed in jeopardy, they were not swayed. Wilberforce succeeded and slavery was abolished in his

6 Romans 8:31
7 Kevin Belmonte, "Steadfast Companions: The Story of Clapham Circle." December 2003

country right before the end of his life. The fortitude and tenacity impregnated in one man gave birth to a new nation.

John Maxwell points out that when a problem is recognized by a few and those few sacrifice to rectify that problem – regardless of the cost—that is when a miracle happens. This is what has changed this nation for the better in the past, and this is what is required in order to incite change in this nation for the future. We cannot hope that lawmakers do what is right or pray that activist judges have a change of heart. Without "we the people" fulfilling our role in government, the Constitution is nothing more than an antiquated mission statement penned over two hundred years ago.

The Constitution is not mere paper from antiquity meant to be seen in museums or read about in history books. It is an active, dynamic document that is as applicable now as it was in its genesis. The same way we reference the Bible in search of spiritual direction, we should reference the Constitution in search of our political freedoms. If we do not use our freedom to defend our freedom, we will lose our freedom.

Nothing appeals to a politician more than intimidated

constituents afraid to open their mouths and use their vote. In order to win this cultural war and change our world, we must change ourselves. Do not wait for someone else to tell you how to help. Take the initiative and help those who are in distress. Do not require your leaders to accomplish for society what you are not willing to accomplish in your own life, church, and community. It is not right to expect change on a greater level if you are not willing to start with the man in the mirror. In order to influence our nation for the good in the greatest of issues, we must be living the gospel in the smallest deeds of our lives. A constant theme of goodness must run deep in all of us in order to set ourselves up as representatives of Christ in the political and social arenas.

Solely enjoying fellowship with like-minded believers does not change the lives of the lost. New relationships must be forged.   Jesus' answer to this situation is expressed in the book of Luke. He was criticized for associating with the sinner, but that did not stop Him. He came "to seek and to save" those who were lost.[8] Unfortunately, many Christians have translated the admonition "to be in the world, but not of it" to mean total and utter separation from the world. Christians

---

8 Luke 19:10

isolate themselves—hoping that the problems in our government and our society will disappear. At best, some are willing to pray about issues, but not willing to tackle them head-on and get involved. That is not to undermine the power of prayer; rather it is being faithful to Biblical principles. God is not going to zap all of our problems away when we pray; He expects us to get busy and change the things we can change. That being said, we must engage our culture in the political debate. To do so successfully, we must be able to express ideas in terms the secular world can understand.

We must relate to the debate. One of the great New Testament examples of a Christian engaging in his surrounding culture is when Paul was in Athens reasoning in the synagogue with the Jews and debating the Greek philosophers in the marketplace.[9] Because of his compelling secular argument for the gospel, he was able to connect with the world around him in terms *they* could understand and identify. He did not throw Scripture at pagans that did not know the Word; instead he used their knowledge and beliefs to turn their attention to God.

Today people feast on satellite news broadcasts, TV, and

9 Acts 17:22-31

radio talk shows. Like the Athenians, our society avidly discusses all the latest ideas and philosophies. But are you able to represent your Christian beliefs confidently when your fellow citizens parrot the latest thing they have heard on Oprah? While some decry daytime talk shows, at least they attempt to address issues that people are thinking about. We as Christians cannot remain mum on these issues; we must stop letting the television set the terms of debate. Become informed! It is not the truth that will set you free; it is the *knowledge* of the truth that will set you free. Learn what that truth is and let your voice be heard.

The purpose of this book is to get you to think about what is happening in your world politically and socially. Letting your light shine means extinguishing the darkness by taking your faith into the secular arena where decisions are being made on issues that affect you and your family. This book is a robust starting point that outlines what is pertinent in our present political culture —while uncovering truths on polarizing issues that currently divide the nation.

Additionally, this book will discuss how we can mobilize a grassroots groundswell of God-believing citizens who can lay siege to the school board, to the city hall, to the state house—all the way to the Congress, the White House and the Supreme Court. This includes getting involved in the election process, and how you, as a voting citizen, can influence public opinion. If you stick to the game plan set forth here, you will be equipped to begin the process of making a difference in the governmental, educational, and moral structures of your world.

As you embark on this journey of political activism, you must always remember that who you are and how you live your daily life will mean more to the people around you than anything you will ever say or any vote you will ever cast. To claim the high moral ground in any political fight, you must be a moral person, living a moral life, fighting a moral cause. You must personify your cause. The solution to our problems is for the Church to come together in unity... to stop fighting each other and start fighting the forces of Satan... to speak for righteousness... to be as bold as a lion... and to take America back one heart at a time, one home at a time, and one city at a time. More than ever the Church of Jesus Christ must let our light shine upon America!

Your Voting Obligation

How far this nation has come since 1776. Then we were striving for greatness; now we are slipping into a moral sewer. Our national foundations are being destroyed as moral men and women sit by and do nothing. Historical revisionists are rewriting American history, attempting to portray our founding fathers as greedy, corrupt, atheistic rebels with nothing to lose. This could not be further from the truth: of the 56 men that gathered in the Pennsylvania State House to draw up the Declaration of Independence, 24 were outstanding lawyers, 9 were wealthy plantation owners, and the 23 remaining were great men of distinction who had a great deal to lose.

These men made a sacred oath to each other, pledging "our lives, our fortunes, and our sacred honor." These men took on the crown of Great Britain; they declared freedom from King George and his taxation without representation. As a result, the King denounced all Americans as "traitors" and ordered them hanged by the neck until dead. Despite the threat these men still signed the Declaration; John Hancock signed his name so large that it would later become one of the most recognizable signatures in history. You think they had nothing to lose?

Wrong! If they lost their war, they would meet their fate by a hangman's rope. If they won, they would endure years of hardship in a struggling nation.

These men signed the Declaration of Independence with ink and paid with their blood. What would happen to these brave men? Thomas McKean of Delaware was so harassed by the British that he was forced to move his family five times in five months. He served the U.S. Congress without pay while his family lived in hiding and endured poverty. Properties that belonged to Clymer, Hall, Gwinnett, Walton, Heyward, Rutledge, and Middleton were all burned to the ground by the British, just to name a few.[10]

Thomas Nelson of Virginia, after whom Thomas Nelson Publishing is named, raised two-million dollars on his own signature to provision our fighting troops. After the war he personally paid back the loans, which wiped out his entire estate, and he was never reimbursed by the government. In the final battle of Yorktown, Nelson's house was occupied by British General Cornwallis; Nelson urged General Washington to fire on his own home in order to defeat the enemy. Washington

---

[10] Paul Harvey, "The Rest of the Story: Our Lives, Our Fortunes, and Our Sacred Honor." 1956
[11] ibid.

complied and the home was totally destroyed. Nelson died homeless, bankrupt, and was buried in an unmarked grave.[11]

John Hart was driven out of his home by the British as he sat at his wife's bedside while she was dying. Their thirteen children fled in all directions in an effort to save themselves. While Hart lived in forests and caves for over a year, his home was burned and his business laid waste. He returned home to find his wife dead and his children and properties gone. He died shortly thereafter of grief and heartache.[12]

The fact of the matter is that these men pledged their lives, their fortunes, and their sacred honor. The price they paid for liberty and freedom is unsurpassable. They gladly gave up their well-established lives in exchange for a freedom they would never fully be able to experience. Is there anything you believe in enough that you would put your reputation and your life in jeopardy? At what point, as a Bible-believing Christian, will you object to the moral corruption being forced upon you, your children and future generations to come?

---

[12] ibid.

*"If we abide by the principles taught in the Bible,
our country will go on prospering and to prosper;
but if we and our posterity neglect its instructions a
nd authority, no man can tell how sudden a
catastrophe may overwhelm us and bury all our
glory in profound obscurity."*

—Daniel Webster
1821

Our founding fathers objected to a tea tax of one-half of one percent, and gave their lives in return. Will we object if our children are routinely indoctrinated in homosexual ideology in our public schools? The homosexual community has come out of the closet; why hasn't the church done the same? Will we take a stand if imperfect babies are being killed in hospitals *after* they are born? Will we protest if the state tells our pastor what he can and cannot say from the pulpit? What if the state assumes "ownership" of children and tells parents how they must raise them—under penalty of losing custody? Will you take action then?

Will we argue if Christian businesses are required to satisfy a quota of gay and lesbian employees? Will the Church cry out if universities refuse to grant degrees to outspoken Christian students? Will we remonstrate when every tenet of our faith is legislated against in Congress? When will we begin to defend our rights and freedoms set forth in our Constitution?

All of the aforementioned are now in process in America. At what point will we have had enough? To make any compromise with the world is to be guilty of treason against God. James states that "a friend of the world is an enemy of God."[13] When will we take action?

Listen to the echo coming from Valley Forge. Look at the American patriot—stained with blood, hungry, barefoot, standing in the snow with his musket firmly grasped. He fought in those conditions and now we are armed with the right to vote, yet we sit at home on Election Day because the weather is bad. That patriot left his family alone and destitute to allow us the freedom of speech, yet we remain silent to avoid political incorrectness or repercussion. He orphaned his crying children in order for us to have a representative government, but through neglect we have allowed that government to become the master of our children and the murderer of the unborn.

---

[13] James 4:4

"We have been assured, Sir, in the Sacred Writings, that 'except the Lord build the House, they labor in vain that build it.' I firmly believe this; and I also believe that without His concurring aid we shall succeed in this political building no better than the builders of Babel."

—Benjamin Franklin
Statement made at the Constitutional Convention,
June 28, 1787

When the Continental Congress came to an impasse, Benjamin Franklin called upon the members of Congress to fall on their knees and ask God for guidance. He said, "We have been assured in the sacred writings (of the Bible) that except the Lord build the house, they labor in vain that built it." Do we labor in vain? Will America endure? In *The Decline and Fall of the Roman Empire*, Edward Gibbon offers six reasons for Rome's collapse: rapid increase in divorce, belittling the sanctity of the home, higher taxes with public monies being wasted, mad craze for hedonistic pleasures, increased spending on armaments while the nation decayed internally, and the decline of faith in God that had become mere form.[14] Does any of this sound familiar? Do you see any reflection of these in our society today?

---

[14] Edward Gibbon, "General Observations on the Fall of the Roman Empire in the West." *(posted on June 15, 1999 http://ancienthistory.about.com)*

In the late eighteenth century Alexander Tyler, a Scottish history professor at the University of Edinborough, had this to say about the fall of the Athenian republic some 2,000 years prior: "A democracy is always temporary in nature; it simply cannot exist as a permanent form of government." "A democracy will continue to exist up until the time that voters discover they can vote themselves generous gifts from the public treasury." Tyler points out that from this moment on, the majority always votes for the candidates who promise the most benefits from the public treasury, the end result being collapse of the democracy with dictatorship soon to follow. [15]

"It is fit and becoming in all people, at times, to acknowledge and revere the Supreme Government of God; to bow in humble submission to His chastisement to confess and deplore their sins and transgressions in the full conviction that the fear of the Lord is the beginning of wisdom; and to pray, with all fervency and contrition, for the pardon of their past offenses, and for a blessing upon their present and prospective action."

—Abraham Lincoln
Declaring a National Day of Prayer and Fasting following
The Battle of Bull Run.

---

[15] Alexander Tyler, "The Fall of a Republic" 1787

Our nation celebrated its 228th birthday in 2004. From the beginning of history, the average age of the world's greatest civilizations has been about two hundred years. During those years, these great nations always progress through the following sequence: from bondage to spiritual faith; from spiritual faith to courage; from courage to liberty; from liberty to abundance; from abundance to complacency; from complacency to apathy; from apathy to dependence; from dependence back into bondage.[16]

Concerning the recent 2000 election, Professor Joseph Olson of Hamline University School of Law suggested that the U.S. is somewhere between the complacency to apathy stage of Professor Tyler's definition of democracy. Olson said, "The map of the territory Bush won was mostly the land owned by the people of this great country, *not* the citizens living in cities in tenements owned by the government and living off the government."[17] Olson noted the fact that this 40 percent of the nation's population has already reached a stage of governmental dependency.

---

[16] ibid.
[17]Joseph Olson, Hamline University School of Law, 2000 (discussing 2000 election statistics—posted on www.retakingamerica.com)

So much is at stake in this election year. We must realize that our freedom is hanging in the balance and apathy threatens to wipe it out all together. America's fate does not lie in the hands of politicians; it lies in the hands of God. Some may wonder why God allows such leaders to rule, but the plain truth is that we, the people, have put godless men in office. God will not cast our vote for us; we still have the free will to sit at home on Election Day.

As we cast our vote, we must vote for people with integrity, character, and a moral foundation. As believers we may say "In God We Trust," but many times we walk into the voting booth and forget Biblical principles. Scripture states that "when the wicked rule, the people mourn!"[18] It goes on to say, "Those who forsake the law praise the wicked, but those who keep the law resist them."[19]

Church, we must take responsibility for our actions. We have repeatedly accepted the filth the world has offered while putting our principles on the back burner. We can no longer sit idly by, convincing ourselves that our vote does not count. The one thing we have in common with the patriots who fought over two hundred years ago is

---

[18] Proverbs 29:2
[19] Proverbs 28:4

the fact that we too are in a war in which the future of America hangs in the balance. That future is our cause, and time is up. God's people must stand up and speak up. The initiative lies solely with us. God responds to our choices. What we do here on earth with prayer and action determines what God can do for us in heaven.

God has given us the authority to make good choices for our land, and we have an obligation to make those choices. The founding fathers risked their lives and sacred honor in order for us to have a voice; we have a moral duty to cry out. Do not think that hope is lost; God will hear the cry of His children. "If my people which are called by My name shall humble themselves, and pray, and seek My face, and turn from their wicked ways; then will I hear from heaven, and will forgive their sin, and will heal their land."[20] We must bear this responsibility and know that the future of America does not lie in the hands of the ungodly... it's in the hands of God's children. It is imperative that we always exercise our right to vote; we have everything to gain and so much to lose.

---

[20] 2 Chronicles 7:14

2

The Family God Intended

"God created man in His own image... male
and female He created them"

—Genesis 1:27

Since the beginning of time, the family has been the
fundamental building block for society. God put man
and woman on this earth and told them to "be fruitful
and multiply."[1] The creation of Adam and Eve is the
greatest evidence supporting the fact that the Almighty
intended the complete family unit to be the basis of

---

[1] Genesis 1:28

human society. Not only is the family a building block for society–but also for procreation, financial security, and even evangelism. Because the family is so foundational for society at large, Satan has done everything in his power to see that the family unit is destroyed. He has attempted anything that demeans the sanctity of the marriage bond or berates the uniqueness of family ties.

Without a family there is no home. Without a positive home life, there is no haven for the strife and pressures of daily living. Satan would love nothing more than for each of us to walk through the valley of death everyday. He attempts to do this by stripping you of the benefits that love and approval of family bring. Satan's attack against the family manifests itself through a variety of spiritual and societal ills. Abortion, abuse, adultery, covetousness, disunity, divorce, enmity, financial troubles, homosexuality, lesbianism, love of money, murder, strife—all are works of the flesh, tools Satan relentlessly uses to attack the fundamental, God-ordained, building block of human relations.

The foundational relationship of the family is the husband and wife. The importance of this divine partnership has been demonstrated through the millennia. After all that is why God created Eve–as a companion suitable for Adam. If Adam could have made it on his own, there would have been no need for Eve. Any student of biography and history can tell you that a man who has achieved great accomplishments has had a strong and mutually supportive wife in his life. Even secular success guru Napoleon Hill, author of one of the great personal goal-achievement books, *Think and Grow Rich*, wrote that one of the major causes of failure in business and personal life is due to the wrong selection of a mate in marriage.[2]

There is a reason why positive contributions made by men without the stabilizing influence of a good woman are very hard to find. Solomon, known as the wisest man of Biblical times, agreed with God's assessment that it was not good for man to be alone. Solomon wrote:

> *There was a man all alone;*
> *he had neither son nor brother.*
> *There was no end to his toil*
> *yet his eyes were not content with his wealth*
> *"For whom am I toiling," he asked,*
> *"and why am I depriving myself of enjoyment?*[3]

---

[2] Napoleon Hill, *Think and Grow Rich*, 1937 p. 103
[3] Ecclesiastes 4:8-7

Just like Adam, the man Solomon described needed a companion, not just to help him through life, but to help him enjoy the fruits of his labor. The husband and wife are the first union necessary to build a family and produce offspring according to God's design. Then the parents and the children together form the basic building block of society. Solomon said that children are a gift from God or a "reward"—the "heritage of the Lord"—and that a man's children are to him like a quiver full of arrows in the hands of a warrior.[4]

Parents have an obligation to raise their children in a godly home according to godly principles, and children have an obligation to honor their parents and care for them in old age, just as the parents cared for the children when they were helpless and dependent. Most of the problems in our society stem from the failure of the family unit to operate as God intended it.

Marriage, by nature, involves a sexual act that unites a man in a woman organically in an act that is potentially procreative. This act of procreation is the actual sense of what the Bible refers to as "one flesh."[5] The reason that marriage, as both nature and God intended it, cannot

4 Psalms 127:3
5 Genesis 2:24

include homosexual relationships is because the act of "one flesh,"–to be fruitful and multiply–is not scientifically possible in a gay relationship.[6] Our government has an incentive in barring homosexual marriage, because marriage is reserved for the begetting and raising of children. The children are tomorrow's society and to expose them to the non-durable and inherently unstable relationships typified by homosexuals would be a threat to our future viability as a successful civilization. Prohibiting homosexual unions is not about meddling in people's private affairs; it is about protecting our future.

We must strive to keep the family unit from becoming extinct and stop at nothing to protect heterosexual marriage. To allow homosexuals to marry would devalue the sanctity of marriage and the stabilizing force that should come with it. A statement recently published in the Netherlands explores the deterioration of marriage in their country following the legalization of same sex marriages. Five noted academics called upon "politicians, academics, and opinion leaders to acknowledge the fact that marriage in the Netherlands is an endangered institution and that many children born out of wedlock are likely to suffer the consequences of

---

6 Robert P. George, *The Clash of Orthodoxies*, 2001, p. 77

that development."[7]

The professors note that, "there are good reasons to believe that the decline in Dutch marriage may be connected to the successful public campaign for the opening of marriage to same-sex couples in the Netherlands."[8] They go on to say that those who have supported these unions also argue in favor of the legal and social separation of marriage from parenting. Likewise, both advocates and opponents agree that same-sex unions would lead to greater approval of unconventional forms of cohabitation.

Since the time that gay marriages have been legal, the Netherlands has witnessed a decline in the number of marriages–from 95,000 in 1990 to 82,000 in 2003. Additionally, the same period experienced an alarming rise in illegitimate births–from one in ten children born out of wedlock to one in three. [9] The professors then went on to discuss that children who are born out of wedlock have a greater chance of encountering problems in psychological development, health, school performance, and quality of future relationships–thus

[7] Professor M. van Mourik, et al., "Statement by Five Dutch Social Science Academics on the Deterioration of Marriage in the Netherlands" *Reformatorisch Dagblad*, 2004
[8] ibid. p.1
[9] ibid. p.1

demoralizing the once strong familial structure the country once relished into a damaging cycle of social decline.

In an interview given by M. Van Mourik, one of the authors of the above statement, he said, "In my view (same-sex marriage) has been an important contributing factor to the decline in the reputation of marriage. It should never have happened"... "We should have had the guts to tell a relatively small group in our society to leave marriage alone."[10] In reference to the marital decline and rise of homosexual marriages, Van Mourik states, "It is no coincidence both take place at the same time. It's a consequence of the rejection of normative schemes that are based on eternal values... and the adoption of a different approach."[11] The serious social consequences that have begun in the Netherlands are just the beginning of a potential world wide fiasco. If we choose to believe that nothing will change by allowing same-sex marriages to take place, we are truly kidding ourselves. Look at what is happening in a small country like the Netherlands; now imagine what could happen if America follows suit.

---

[10] Addy de Jong, "Interview with Dutch Scholars on Marriage" *Reformatorisch Dagblad*, 2004
[11] ibid. p. 2

What is so bad about gay rights?

"Gay liberation was founded... on a 'sexual brotherhood of promiscuity,' and any abandonment of that promiscuity would amount to a 'communal betrayal of gargantuan proportions.'"

—Gabriel Rotello, gay author
-noting the perspective of the gay community

Empirical and Moral Arguments

Many homosexual activists such as Andrew Sullivan, a young, gay, British Roman Catholic, allege that homosexual conduct is virtuous, stable, and reserves sex for loving monogamous relationships while embracing other, "family values."[12]   While this ideal may seem appealing to those who wish to close their eyes at the homosexual agenda, it is empirically untrue. For instance, Dr. John R. Diggs, a physician, claims that it is his, "duty to assess behaviors for their impact on health and well being. When something is beneficial, such as exercise, good nutrition, or adequate sleep, it is my duty to recommend it." He goes on further to say, "Likewise,

---

12 Robert P. George, "The Clash of Orthodoxies: Law, Religion and Morality in Crisis." 2001, p., 264

when something is harmful, such as smoking, overeating, alcohol or drug abuse, it is my duty to discourage it."[13] Therefore, as a doctor of medicine, it is his "duty to inform patients of the health risks of gay sex, and to discourage them from indulging in harmful behavior." Nevertheless Dr. Diggs goes on to discuss that due to "the nature of sex" among homosexuals, sexually transmitted diseases, most of which are virtually non-existent in the heterosexual population, are reaching epidemic proportions in some regions.

In a wide field study of homosexual white males, 75 percent of self-identified gay men disclosed to having sex with more than 100 different males in their lifetime, while 28 percent claimed more than 1,000.[14] Both gay advocates and critics alike agree that fidelity is rare, if not non-existent in homosexual relationships. Michelangelo Signorile, homosexual author and activist, defines what successful commitment is in a gay relationship:

> For these men the term "monogamy" simply doesn't necessarily mean sexual exclusivity... the term "open relation-

[13] John R. Diggs, Jr., M.D., "The Health Risks of Gay Sex." Corporate Resource Council, 2002, p.1
[14] ibid.,p.1

ship" has for a great many gay men come to have one specific definition: A relationship in which the partners have sex on the outside often, put away their resentment and jealousy, and discuss their outside sex with each other, or share sex partners.[15]

William Aaron, a former homosexual, shines some light on why monogamy is not found in "committed" homosexual relationships:

In the gay life, fidelity is almost impossible. Since part of the compulsion of homosexuality seems to be a need on the part of the homophile to "absorb" masculinity from his sexual partners, he must be constantly on the lookout for [new partners]. Consequently the most successful homophile "marriages" are those where there is an arrangement between the two to have affairs on the side while maintaining the semblance of permanence in their living arrangement.[16]

---

[15] Michelangelo Signorile, *Life Outside* New York: Harper Collins, 1997 p. 213

[16] William Aaron, *Straight* New York: Bantam Books, 1972 p. 208

We must understand that granting homosexual marriage serves as nothing more than governmental approval of promiscuous behavior and a vehicle for disease to run rampant.

When something is detrimental to our overall health and well being, a doctor feels it his or her obligation to cry out—in that same manner Almighty God cries out against homosexuality. The Lord instructs that, "If a man also lies with mankind, as he lieth with a woman, both of them have committed an abomination: they shall surely be put to death; their blood [shall be] upon them."[17] God does everything for a specific reason; His forbidding homosexuality is not done arbitrarily. He does so in order to protect humanity from sickness, disease, and a life of torment that leads to premature death.

Given these empirical facts, are these statistics really something that we want to embrace? Given the state of our society now, we have already learned that fewer marriages and out-of-wedlock births are not the keys to a healthy civilization. The reason our nation has laws regarding marriage in the first place is because society has an obligation to care and nurture its children. Not only is marriage being redefined and destroyed, but now

---

[17] Leviticus 20:13

we want to replace the care and nurturing of children with personal satisfaction and desire.

For example, Gretchen Ritter, a women's studies professor at the University of Texas, alleges that stay-at-home moms deliver damaging effects to men, women, children and society as a whole.[18] She states that:

> The stay-at-home mom is bad for society. It tells employers that women who marry and have children are at risk of withdrawing from their careers... full time mothering is also bad for children. It teaches them that the world is divided by gender... the more stay-at-home mothers there are, the more schools and libraries will neglect the needs of working parents, and the more professional mothers, single mothers, working-class mothers, and lesbian mothers will feel judged.[19]

Not only does this perspective berate the nurturing of children, it also condemns the women who do it. Instead of applauding those who care for our future

---

[18] transcript of Gretchen Ritter posted on Break Point with Charles Colson. "A Strange Take on Stay-at-Home Moms" (Commentary #040727) July 27, 2004
[19] ibid.

generations, we are beginning to blame them for our social and societal shortcomings.

The problem with our nation today is that we have gradually become tolerant of homosexual agendas being forced upon us. As J. Budziszewski points out:

> The list of what we are required to approve of is growing ever longer. Consider just the domain of sexual practices, first we were to approve of sex before marriage, then without marriage, now against marriage. ... first with one, then with a series, now with a crowd; first with the other sex, then with the same; first between adults, then between children, then between adults and children.[20]

While we are aware that sex between adults and children has yet to be added to the list, it shall come to pass. The irony of the situation at hand is that the liberal-left in this nation has long held that sexual behavior is beyond the reach of governmental influence. While they feel the need to legislate welfare, religion,

---

[20] J. Budziszewski, "The Revenge of Conscience: Politics and the Fall of Man." 1999, p.20

environment and race issues, they have for the most part claimed that government should remain powerless when it comes to regulating sex.[21]

How the tides have turned. Leaders in the homosexual community have consented that the typical homosexual lifestyle consists of volatile relationships marked by nameless affairs and multiple partners. Due to the fact that this cultivates social instability and a wave of diseases, there are those who now allege that permitting homosexuals to legally marry would promote them to commit to one another in stable monogamous relationships.[22] Despite past attempts in accusing the religious conservative desires to regulate sexual morality, liberals now endeavor to do just that.

Constitutional Argument:

"We know that the law is good if one uses it properly. We also know that law is made not for the righteous but for lawbreakers and rebels, the ungodly and sinful, the unholy and irreligious... for adulterers and perverts...and whatever else is contrary to the

---

[21] Dr. Norman Geisler & Frank Turek, "Legislating Morality." 1998 p.129
[22] ibid. p.130

sound doctrine that conforms to the glorious gospel of the blessed God, which he entrusted to me." [23]

America cannot continue to look the other way while homosexual activists hijack the judicial system in this nation. In the current debates, homosexuals are attempting to usurp the Constitutional protection offered in the 14th Amendment. This amendment, one of the three "freedman's laws" ratified after the Civil War, was drafted to integrate and further protect the newly freed slaves in our nation. The 14th Amendment is the lengthiest and most complex of the three, and within this amendment there are several clauses. The Equal Protection Clause is one of significance for our purposes. The clause reads as follows: "No state shall deny to any person within its jurisdiction equal protection of the laws."[24]

At first sight one may assume that this serves as carte blanche for courts to okay homosexual marriage, citing that to deny a couple the right to marry is to deny them equal protection of the laws. However, this is not the case. The Supreme Court holds that the Equal

---

[23] I Timothy 1:8-11
[24] Constitution of the United States of America, Equal Protection Clause of the 14th Amendment, 1868

Protection Clause goes no further than protecting "invidious discrimination;" put plainly, this means random and unreliable discrimination that has no rational basis.[25] Therefore, *rational* discrimination *is* by-all-means constitutionally permissible. To say discrimination must be rational is to say that there is a rational reason, related to a state interest, in imposing discrimination. For instance, it is a law that young adults cannot legally drink alcohol until they reach the age of twenty-one. While some youngsters may cry "age discrimination," the real precept behind such a law is to protect society from the effects of underage drinking and the irresponsible and sometimes dangerous situations that arise with it.

So then, what is a rational reason for mandating that marriage only be recognized between a man and a woman? Heterosexual marriage is absolutely necessary in order to maintain a viable society. Maggie Gallagher, a fellow at the Ethics and Public Policy Center, has this to say about supporting traditional marriage, and offering spousal benefits to alternate forms of cohabitants: that it, "...further erodes the status and practice of marriage, ultimately reducing the well-being of children, increasing taxpayer costs, and retarding work force

---

[25] *Williamson v. Lee Optical Co.*, 348 U.S. 483 (1955)

productivity and economic progress."[26] This is enough of a compelling and *rational* reason to prohibit same-sex unions. Lawmakers could make their decisions based on secular empirical evidence, without ever having to use the Church as their defense. Instead they are permitting the homosexual community, along with activist judges, to hijack the court system.

The highest form of legal protection for minority groups offered by the Supreme Court is reserved for cases involving *racial* discrimination. Usually in court it is the offended party that has the task of proving that a wrong has been committed toward them. However, in racial discrimination cases the burden of proof lies with the government—meaning the onus lies on the government to prove that an injustice is being committed—and if so it is their responsibility to rectify the situation. Since it is enticing for aggrieved parties to seek out this protection, due to the fact that the court is the one that has to prove the offended partie's case—the Supreme Court made it clear that this protection can only be afforded to "those groups that constitute discrete and insular minorities that have experienced a history of unequal treatment and lack of political power."[27] The homosexual

---

[26] Maggie Gallagher "Why Supporting Marriage Makes Business Sense"
Corporate Resource Council, 2002 p. 10
[27] ibid. 2 p.622

community is trying to portray themselves as this "insular minority" in order to redeem this protection from the Court. However, this does not describe the homosexual community; while they are a minority, less than 3 percent of the population, they are a minority by choice, and they are anything but politically powerless.[28]

Despite what the politically correct may claim, one is not born a homosexual. There is no "gay" gene, and as was reported in a medical study, "lesbian women were 4.5 times more likely to have had more than 50 lifetime male partners than heterosexual women; and 93 percent of women who identified themselves as lesbian reported a history of sex with men."[29] If homosexuality is not a choice, rather a condition one is born with, then why undulate between male and female sex partners? Race, however, is not a choice. One does not wake up one day and decide that he or she wants to become African-American, you either are or you aren't. Regardless of that fact, there should be no need to answer the question, "Can one be born a homosexual?" That answer should have no bearing on what the law *should* be; laws do not excuse conduct on the basis of

---

[28] ibid. Diggs, p.3
[29] Catherine Hutchinson, et al., "Characteristics of Patients with Syphilis Attending Baltimore STD Clinics," Archives of Internal Medicine, 151:511-516, p.513 (1991)

genetic predisposition.[30] We cannot allow the gay community to run rampant in our courthouses masking their agendas as violations of their civil rights.

As for the term "politically powerless," these are words hardly used to describe the homosexual community. For instance, in February 2004 the Massachusetts Supreme Judicial Court, in a 4-3 ruling, cleared the way for homosexual couples to marry; even though homosexual make up less than two percent of the city's population. This example of what is happening in Massachusetts, along with four other states, is nothing more than a clear and obvious case of the courts overruling the majority opinion of the people. In 1999, civil unions were passed in Vermont and five years later we have moved on to marriage? Does this sound like a group of "politically powerless" people? Let me paint a picture of a "historically disadvantaged and politically powerless" people.

In *Brown v. Board of Education*, in 1954, the Supreme Court overturned their "separate but equal doctrine" that had been the previous standard for treatment of African-Americans since 1896. This "doctrine" mandated that whites and blacks were to be treated completely separately, but in an equal manner (bear in mind the "freedman's laws" were ratified in 1868). As anyone can tell you, only half of that order was followed. African-Americans remained *completely* separated from Caucasians, but they were not treated equally. Not until six decades had passed was this ruling overturned in the *Brown* case. It wasn't until a young girl's parents had had enough and demanded their daughter be able to receive a racially integrated education.[31] Even then, the court still waited another year before determining how to begin integration. Still, it can further be argued that in certain regions of our nation today, African-Americans and Caucasians continue to live in separate societies.

Here we have a group of people who have been one of the most historically persecuted in our nation. Amendments were passed in the 1860's to give them freedom, yet they were still to be treated "separate" from society. A century later, despite their "freedom," they were still begging to be treated as equals; and sadly enough, in certain places, racism remains. The real travesty in this situation is the fact that the homosexual community is successfully commandeering these civil rights for themselves, alleging that *they* are the ones who have been persecuted. If the courts acquiesce to the

---

31 *Brown v. Board of Education of Topeka Kansas*, 347 U.S. 483 (1954)

homosexual agenda, they owe the African-American population of this country an apology.

Amendment protecting Heterosexual Marriage:

In the United States today, each state governs its own marriage laws. The legal provisions themselves number into the hundreds in each state and more than 1,049 at the federal level. These laws cover every conceivable aspect of social interaction.[32]   One aspect of our law is that, under the Constitution, states are not allowed to legislate against each other.   The Constitution states that, "full faith and credit shall be given in each state to the... judicial proceedings of every other state."[33]   So why not follow the politicians' advice and "leave it up to the states" to decide? This is not an option due to the "full faith and credit" clause in the Constitution. This clause in Article IV requires all states to recognize marriages conducted in each state—so if one state legalizes homosexual marriages, the remaining 49 states are required to also recognize that marriage.

---

[32] "Legal Marriage Court Cases—A Timeline"
[33] United States Constitution, Article IV, Section I

Although the Defense of Marriage Act (DOMA) presumably prevents this from occurring, it is imperative that the federal courts not be permitted to rule DOMA unconstitutional. If they do so, then one state's allowance is all it takes in order to start a chain reaction of homosexual unions throughout the nation. We must urge our representatives to pass a bill that would prevent the federal courts from ever doing such a thing. Homosexual relationships cannot approximate what the family does. The disease, volatility, promiscuity and infidelity that accompany these relationships are a recipe for the destruction of society. Society, through government, has an interest in encouraging marriage and in preserving its uniqueness under law in order to guarantee our future.

While the DOMA is a sound starting point in our effort to maintain the sanctity of marriage, the only way to ensure our commitment to marriage and our commitment to a healthy society is to mandate that our nation pass an amendment stating that the United States will only recognize a marriage between a man and a woman. Our nation has been taken over by federal activist judges who are at war with the will of the people. They are trying to force same-sex "marriages" in a nation where over seventy percent of the population is against it. The homosexual community averages between one and three percent of the population, and they are trying to dominate society.[34] If Christians are over seventy-five percent strong... why do our voices remain silent? Instead why don't we use our vote to declare our position? While homosexuals and activists alike have told America to "stay out of the bedroom," they are the ones pulling their bedrooms out into society. The gay and lesbian community does not want tolerance—they want endorsement.

Neutrality is not a sufficient weapon for this battle. Homosexuals are not taking a neutral position; they want to impose their morality on society at large. Paula Ettlebrick, the former legal director of the Lambda Legal Defense and Education Fund, has stated, "Being queer is more than setting up house, sleeping with a person of the same gender, and seeking state approval for doing so... being queer means pushing the parameters of sex, sexuality, and family, and in the process transforming the very fabric of society."[35] This is the antithesis of a neutral position; we must realize that equal respect of opposite sides cannot exist. Although some pluralists have

[34] John R. Diggs Jr., M.D. "The Health Risks of Gay Sex," Corporate Resource Council, 2002, p.3
[35] Paula Ettelbrick, quoted in William B. Rubinstein, "Since When is Marriage a Path to Liberation?" *Lesbians, Gay Men, and the Law*, New York: The New Press, 1993 pp. 398-400.

suggested using "equal respect for each other" as a starting point rather than an ending point in understanding our differences, this is nothing more than a recipe for the illogical. [36]

Marriage is not what the law says it is. Marriage has been around since the beginning of time. Ever since God gave Eve to Adam and called her his wife, marriage has been a God-ordained institution.[37]   God created marriage, not laws, not the framers, not the Constitution; rather it is a holy union established by the Almighty.   We must stop exhausting words like *tolerance* and *acceptance* and start using words like *morality* and *monogamy*. It is our moral obligation to ourselves and the future of society to stop a union that God never intended.

---

[36] ibid. Budziszewski p.9
[37] Genesis 2:20-24

3

Defending the Defenseless

"I've noticed those *for* abortion
have already been born."

—Ronald Reagan

Abortion

Personhood is properly defined by membership in the
human species, not by a stage of development within
that species.[1] Yet ever since the Supreme Court held in

---

[1] Randy Alcorn. " Pro Life Answers to Pro Choice Arguments" p.57

Roe v. Wade, that women were free to abort their unborn children, society has attempted to redefine personhood altogether. In *Roe*, the court held that within the first and second trimesters of pregnancy abortions could basically be performed at the mother's will. The court went on to say that the individual states can regulate third trimester abortions, if they so choose, as long as provisions are made for both life and health.[2] The interesting question is, if unborn babies are not people, then why regulate abortion at all? Why did the court so painstakingly outline what a woman could and could not do in terms of aborting a pregnancy? They did so because the action is not without controversy; they did so because it was a human life that hung in the balance.

Abortion is one of Satan's most sinister machinations: it strikes against the very heart and fiber of what a family is about. For the mother and father of a child to petition a doctor to extinguish its life goes against everything motherhood and parenthood represent. The abortion movement is nothing less than an attempt to format social change to "liberate" women from the obligations, cares, and responsibilities of motherhood. The

2 Lee Epstein and Thomas G. Walker. " Constituional Law for a Changing America" p.432

ubiquitous argument is that "it is the women's right to choose" and prohibiting abortion restricts her freedom to make that choice. The freedom to choose what? What about the unborn child's freedom? What about their lifetime of choices that is being robbed of them? It is hazardous, for the human race as a whole, when people in power are able to determine whether other, less powerful lives are meaningful.[3]

Although *Roe v. Wade* decimated the civil rights of an entire class of people, this was not the first time they had done so. As previously discussed, the Court, as well as society as a whole, has had a history of persecuting African Americans. In years immediately prior to the Civil War, the Supreme Court decreed in *Dred Scott v. Sanford* that blacks were not as "human" as a white person and therefore could be bought and sold as property.[4] During World War II the Supreme Court decided it *was* constitutional to disenfranchise Japanese-Americans of their property and to contain them in what were fundamentally concentration camps for the duration of the war. Those decisions, along with *Roe v. Wade*, constitute the trinity of Supreme Court disaster. As the previously mentioned case held, among other

---

3 ibid. p.57
4 Scott v. Sanford 19 How (60. U.S.) 393 (1857)

things, that an unborn child was not a person and therefore not protected by the Fourteenth Amendment to the Constitution. The Amendment says that a state shall not "deprive any person of life, liberty, or property, without due process of law; nor deny to any person within its jurisdiction the equal protection of the laws."

Justice Blackmun's majority opinion stated: "If this suggestion of personhood is established, the appellant's case, of course, collapses, for the fetus' right to life would then be guaranteed specifically by the Amendment." The Court went on to say, however, that it was persuaded "that the word 'person,' as used in Fourteenth Amendment, does not include the unborn."[5] It came down to a matter of nomenclature with the court; the justices held that a fetus was not a person. Randy Alcorn points out that, "like *toddler* and *adolescent*, the terms embryo and fetus do not refer to nonhumans, but to humans at particular stages of development."[6]

Social liberals, who pride themselves in engineering society, would love nothing more than to dissolve the traditional family structure. They believe childbearing,

---

5 Roe v. Wade (1973) cited earlier
6 ibid. p. 46

which is the most *womanly* of functions, represents everything feminists and social revolutionaries wish to eliminate. As quoted by Planned Parenthood of America, "To impose a law defining a fetus as a 'person,' is granting it rights equal to that or superior to a woman's; a thinking, feeling, conscious human being-is arrogant and absurd. It only serves to diminish women."[7] The thinking behind this precept is that if a woman can have the option of sex without pregnancy, then the woman is freed from the domination of men and from the obligations of a home and a family.

Protecting the lives of the unborn is not the male-dominated society's attempt to curtail a woman's potential. The pro-life movement is not centered on keeping women in the home "barefoot and pregnant," they are solely about protecting human life. In Proverbs 31, the ideal picture of a woman is presented. Not only does this woman have a husband and children, but many verses are dedicated to portraying the woman as a powerful entrepreneur.

---

[7] Planned Parenthood Federation of America, Inc. "Nine Reasons Why Abortions are Legal" p.2, 1989

*"She selects wool and flax and works with eager
hands. She is like the merchant ships bringing her
food from afar... she considers a field and buys it;
out of her earnings she plants a vineyard. She sets
about her work vigorously; her arms are strong for
her tasks. She sees that her trading is profitable,
and her lamp does not go out at night."*

—Proverbs 31:13-14,16-18

Even two thousand years ago, "the woman who had it
all" not only had a husband and a family; but she also
had a life of her own that she found fulfilling for herself.

There is no larger issue in America today and no debate
that more clearly draws the line in the sand between
right and wrong than abortion. It is a line that demarks
a difference as dramatic and obvious as the line between
light and darkness. Ever since that fateful day in 1973,
when the Supreme Court held abortions were legal a
war has raged between the forces of light; those who
stand for preserving the lives of the most innocent and
defenseless among us; and the powers of darkness, those
who in the name of "reproductive freedom" argue for
the right to end the lives of children they deem to be an
inconvenience.

God has created all of us as free moral agents. We have the ability to choose between right and wrong. In Scripture, speaking through Moses, God told His people:

"I call heaven and earth as witnesses today against you, that I have set before you life and death, blessing and cursing. Therefore choose life, so that both you and your descendants may live."

—Deuteronomy 30:19

Although God has given us the ability to make our own choices, He is quite explicit about what choice we should make: "choose life." Despite God's direction, Americans today have *not* been choosing life in staggering numbers. Every year nearly a million-and-a-half abortions are performed in the United States alone; well over thirty-seven million babies have been wantonly destroyed since our Supreme Court rewrote the abortion laws nationwide. [8]

---

[8] Stuart M. Butler and Kim R. Holmes. "Issues 2000: The Candidates Briefing Book." The Heritage Foundation, 200 p. 212

Partial Birth and More

"As any sin passes through its stages; from temptation, to toleration, to approve its name is first euphemized, then avoided, then forgotten... first we were to approve of killing unborn babies, then babies in the process of birth, next came newborns with physical defects, now newborns in perfect health."

— J. Budziszewski

While Americans have blatantly not chosen life in this matter of abortion, now with our medical prowess, Americans are choosing as to what method they wish to use in ending the lives of their unborn children. James Watson, the Nobel-prize laureate who discovered the structure of DNA, proposed that "parents of newborns be granted a grace period which they may have their babies killed."[9] Furthermore in 1994 a committee of the American Medical Association suggested harvesting organs from sick babies even before they die.[10] While this may seem like something out of fiction, read the following descriptions of exactly how all of these torturous procedures are executed.

---

[9] J. Budzisewski. "The Revenge of Conscience: Politics and the Fall of Man." 1999 p.21
[10] ibid p.21

"For you created me in my inmost being;
you knit me in my mother's womb."

—Psalms 139:13

The most common technique used in first trimester abortion is called suction aspiration, or "vacuum curettage."[11] This procedure consists of a powerful suction tube while a sharp cutting edge is inserted into the womb through the dilated cervix. After insertion the suction "dismembers the body of the developing baby and tears the placenta from the wall of the uterus, sucking blood, amniotic fluid, placental tissue, and fetal parts into a collection bottle."[12]

When babies in the womb are as old as 24 weeks, a Dilation and Evacuation can be used. Via this method, "forceps with sharp metal jaws are used to grasp parts of the developing baby, which are then twisted and torn away; this continues until the child's entire body is removed from the womb. Because the baby's skull has often hardened to bone by this time, it must sometimes

---

11 Phillip G. Stubblefield. "First and Second Trimester Abortion" *Gynecologic and Obstetric Surgery,* ed. David H. Nichols (Baltimore: Mosby, 1993) p.1016
12 U.S. Center for Disease Control (CDC), "Abortion Surveillance: Preliminary Data-United States, 1991" Morbidity and Mortality Report, Vol. 43, No, 1994, p. 43

be compressed or crushed to facilitate removal."[13]

Lastly and quite possibly the *most* disconcerting of all the methods is what is known as the Partial-Birth Abortion, or a D&X (a.k.a. dilation and extraction) abortion. This procedure is used in women that are 20 to 32 weeks pregnant-sometimes even later into pregnancy. During this procedure, the abortionist, guided by ultrasound, reaches into the uterus, grabs the baby's leg with forceps, and pulls the baby into the birth canal, feet first, and begins to pull the baby's body out of the mother while the head is left face down in the birth canal. (It is important to note, during this portion of the procedure, the baby is still alive.) When the baby's body is outside of the vagina and only the head remains face down inside the mother, the abortionist thrusts a blunt, curved pair of scissors into the base of the skull and then opens the scissors to enlarge the wound. After a hole has been made, the scissors are removed and a suction catheter is placed into the hole as it sucks out the baby's brain and skull contents. After the skull is collapsed, the baby is then fully delivered from the mother.[14]

---

[13] Warren M. Hern, M.D., *Abortion Practice* (Philadelphia: J.B. Lipincott Company, 1984), pp.153-154

[14] Dr. Martin Haskell. "Second Trimester D&X, 20 Wks and Beyond" National Abortion Federation: Second Trimester Abortion: From Every Angle 1992 pp. 29-31

Dr. Martin Haskell, who describes the partial birth procedure above, said that he had personally performed 700 of these abortions.[15] Although some pro-choice activists would like us to believe otherwise, partial births are more common than we would think. In a news release on November 1, 1995, the Planned Parenthood Federation of America claimed "The procedure, dilation and extraction (a.k.a. partial birth) is extremely rare and done only in cases when the woman's life is in danger or in cases of extreme fetal abnormality." This allegation has been echoed by pro-choice advocates everywhere, and many people believe that there was truth behind such claims. This dialogue was rendered moot when the executive director of the National Coalition of Abortion Providers, Ron Fitzsimmons, publicly admitted he "lied through [his] teeth" when he alleged that partial birth abortions were a rare procedure performed only in extreme and rare situations.[16] Fitzsimmons went on to state that "he intentionally misled in previous remarks... because he feared that the truth would damage the cause of abortion rights. Additionally he admitted that although he still supported the procedure, he had conceded that "It is a form of killing. You're ending a life."[17]

---

15 ibid pp.15-16
16 David Stout, An *Abortion Rights Advocate Says He Lied About Procedure*, New York Times, Feb. 26,1997
17 ibid.

Another argument that abortion advocates attempt to advance is that the fetus cannot feel the pain of these abortions as they are being performed. The truth is that not only can the unborn feel pain, they can feel it more acutely than if they were outside the womb. An expert on fetal pain, Dr. Anad, wrote in his report to the U.S. Federal Court that, "scientific evidence converge to support the conclusion that the human fetus can experience pain from 20 weeks gestation and possibly as early as 16 weeks of gestation."[18] He then went on to say that the pain felt by a fetus is "more intense than perceived by term newborns or older children" and that the process of partial-birth abortion would result in "prolonged and intense pain experienced by the human fetus."[19] We must realize that these procedures are happening in our country, not Nazi Germany, and they are taking place more often than we think. It was reported by the National Director of Abortion Providers that, in 1997 alone, between three to five thousand partial birth abortions had been conducted.[20]

[18] Dr. Kanawaljeet S. Anad. (fetal pain expert) *Excerpt from report to U.S. Federal Court regarding Partial Birth Act.* January 15,2004, pp. 5-6
[19] ibid.
[20] Douglas Johnson. "The Partial-Birth Abortion Act-Misconceptions and Realities," 2003 p.3

*"Blessed are you among women, and blessed
is the child you will bear! But why am I so favored,
that the mother of my Lord should come to me? As
soon as the sound of your greeting reached my ears,
the baby in my womb leaped for joy."*

—Luke 1:42-44

Another argument that the abortion advocates would
like us to believe is abortion is allowable due to the fact
that the "fetus" is inside a woman's body and dependant
upon that woman's life for survival; then the fetus is not
self-sustaining and therefore cannot be considered a life.
However, what happens when a woman has a newborn
for that matter? If a parent were to leave a one year old
in a house by him or herself, could he or she be self-
sustaining? Surely not; a child is dependent upon the
parent for years after birth in order to survive; that
dependency does not end as soon as they are no longer
in the womb.

Additionally, there have been cases where children were
born uncharacteristically early and still survived outside
the womb. This was the case with Courtney Jackson,
who was born after just 23 weeks into gestation; she

was born weighing 460 grams, was 11 inches long, had eight teaspoons of blood in her entire body, and had a heart that was not any bigger than an acorn.[21] While the odds were stacked against her, the little girl pulled through and lives a normal life today. Pictures of little Courtney's birth should be hanging on the wall of every abortion clinic; it would be a face to the life that they were about to end.

Abortion ends a life, a human life, and it is as simple, and as wrong, and as hellish as that. Abortion prevents a future teacher from teaching, stops a future coach from leading, it keeps a doctor from healing, and it guarantees that a future writer will never get a chance to inspire. Abortion is not only a sin against the infant; abortion is also a sin against the future of humanity. Over 40 million putative U.S. citizens have been legally murdered in this country. When will it stop?

---

21 Susan Schindehette. "Against All Odds," *People Magazine*, July 19, 2004, pp. 61-62

Stem Cell and the Slippery Slope that Follows...

*"So why do things get worst so fast...
the usual explanation is that conscience is
weakened by neglect. Once a wrong is done,
the next wrong comes more easily."*

—J. Budziszewski

Is the destruction of human embryos in fact killing a human being? Why wouldn't it be? The ovum and the sperm (gamete) are a product of the male and female body; they are reproductive cells that are *able* to unite with another for sexual reproduction. However, when those two components successfully unite inside a woman's body, a fertilized egg or embryo is created. Embryos are independent entities; they are defined as "unborn offspring." One can think of an embryo as a very tiny person, not a potential one; rather it is an actual life. Whatever *is* human must be human from its beginnings.[22] Whoever is an adult now, is the same being that was once a teenage adolescent, and before that a toddler, and before that an infant, and before that a fetus, and before that an embryo.[23]

---

[22] ibid. Alcorn. p. 54
[23] Robert P. George, "Don't Destroy Human Life," *The Wall Street Journal*, Monday, July 30, 2001

Stem cells are actually cells that, "are isolated from human embryos that are a few days old." The National Institute of Health states that "cells from these embryos can be used to create pluripotent stem cell "lines" or cell cultures that can be grown indefinitely in the laboratory. Pluripotent stem cell lines have also been developed from fetal tissue that is older than eight weeks old."[24] To put this in laymen's terms, tissue is harvested from a two month old fetus for research purposes.

The proposed idea is to create human embryos in a lab in order to harvest stem cells from them. A fertilized egg is considered "totipotent, meaning that its potential is total; it gives rise to all the different types of cells in the body."[25] The National Institute of Health makes an interesting point here; it says that a "fertilized egg" or embryo has total potential to give rise to all of the different cell types in the human body. This is because an embryo *is* human! Modern science shows us that embryos are "whole living members of the human species, who are capable of directing from within their own integral organic functioning development into that through the fetal, infant, child and adolescent stages of life and ultimately into adulthood."[26]

---

[24] http://stemcells.nih.gov/info/faqs.asp#whatare The official *National Institutes of Health* resource for stem cell research
[25] ibid. NIH
[26] ibid. George p. 1

Robert P. George, a professor of jurisprudence at Princeton University, points out that in current debates, "the question whether a human embryo is a human being is usually ignored or evaded."[27] He uses an interesting word here, as J. Budziszewski points out that "avoidance" is a sign that things in society are getting worse.[28] He cites an example of where avoidance fits in this process of a deteriorating culture.

> "A colleague of mine tells me that some of his fellow scholars call child molestation "in intergenerational intimacy": that's *euphemism.* A goodhearted editor once tried to talk me out of using the term "sodomy": that's *avoidance.* My students don't know the word "fornication" at all: that's *forgetfulness.*"[29]

Will our society stop at nothing short of infanticide? George points out that some proponents of stem cell research concede that the embryos are indeed human beings.[30] So what does this do to the abortion argument? If embryos are human beings; then how is it abortions

---

[27] ibid. George p.1
[28] ibid. Budzisaewski p.20
[29] ibid. George p.1
[30] ibid. George p.1

are *not* considered murder? Peter Singer, a Princeton professor and a utilitarian, does not believe that there is a principle of inherent human dignity that prohibits killing some people for the sake of the supposed "greater good," thus there is no moral repugnance in mutilating human embryos for their stem cells.[31] That being said utilitarians, and those who are like minded, would see no reason not to kill human beings at any stage in their life so long as it serves the "greater good" of society.[32]

So then where does it end? Just because medical science has the capacity to do something does not mean it should be done. The "Baby Doe" case in 1982 is just one example of the unstoppable slippery slope that has reared its ugly head since *Roe v. Wade*. A baby girl was born in Indiana with Down syndrome and an esophageal abnormality that could be easily remedied by surgery. However, her parents felt too burdened by the child's existence and elected against the surgery. Instead they asked their physician not to administer any food or water to their child. As a result the child's lungs were slowly digested by gastric juices while she starved to death. While one would hope that the courts would intervene on such matters, this did not occur. The

---

[31] ibid. George
[32] ibid. George p.1

Indiana Supreme Court ruled that this fell in the category of the parent's right to privacy, and no repercussions were made.[33] So now that our society has no problem killing embryos, fetuses, or children, what will come next?

Marjorie Nighbert suffered a stroke in April 1994. She was 83 years old, and as a result of her stroke was left with disabilities, including difficulty swallowing, which is a common side effect of stroke victims. In order for Marjorie to live, a feeding tube needed to be inserted in order to nourish and hydrate her—however the tube was later removed against her will. This was because in 1992 Marjorie entrusted her brother with power of attorney in her health care matters. Upon his direction, his sister was not to have a feeding tube. As a result Marjorie began to beg those caring for her to give her food and water and they refused. It was only after a staff member had confessed to a priest what was happening that Florida's Health and Rehabilitation Services were called in to intervene. In a court, a judge ruled that Marjorie should not be fed, due to the fact that she was not competent to ask for food. She died April 1995, while the employee who tried to save her was fired.[34]

---

[33] PJ King. "Targeting the Vulnerable," Sept. 2000
http://www.pregnatpause.org
[34] ibid. p.1

This is not the only time a travesty like this has occurred. Burt Kiezer, Dutch physician and author, reacted in a similar manner when one of his nursing home residents began to choke on her food; "he shot her full of morphine and waited for her to die."[35] While advocates of such procedures refer to this as "the ultimate civil liberty,"[36] accepting this as a reasonable way to confront death is pregnant with eternal ramifications. The same way that God is in control of creating life, is the same way that He is in control of ending life. Jesus is our ultimate example of suffering. His commitment to complete the will of His Father, regardless of the personal cost, is the antithesis of opting for the easy way out of pain or difficulty by means of suicide, with or without a physician.

When it comes to the suffering of others, our example is the Good Samaritan who came upon a man who was suffering from exposure, and had extreme loss of blood and was completely unable to fend for himself.[37] The Good Samaritan was a consummate caregiver, not a "mercy killer". He did not bash the dying man's brains out for the sake of convenience, allowing him to

---

[35] ibid. Budziszewski p.21
[36] Derek Humphrey, founder of the Hemlock Society and president of ERGO! (Euthanasia Research and Guidance Organization) http://finalexit.org
[37] Luke 10:25-37

"humanely" pass into eternity. Instead he nursed him back to health because the Samaritan's actions were motivated by his eternal values. Of the kindness that the Samaritan offered to the man in need, Jesus tells us to "go and do likewise."[38]

For a physician to act in any way other than to alleviate a person's physical pain and emotional distress, or for a physician to assist his or her patient out of a transitory situation with a permanent solution of death is completely antithetical to his or her Hippocratic Oath. That no one should have the right to take the life of another, born or unborn, is an ancient principle of medicine. The Hippocratic Oath, first formulated as a sworn rule of conduct for doctors in ancient Greece about 2,400 years ago, says, "I will give no deadly medicine to any one if asked, nor suggest such counsel; and in a like matter I will not give a women a pessary to induce an abortion."[39] If Hippocrates, a pagan physician who believed in various mythological gods, demi-gods, and goddesses-knew that it was wrong to take a life, what defense do we have today after the intervening of two millennia of research and learning?

---

[38] Luke 10:37
[39] The Hippocratic Oath (Original Version), by the Hippocrates of Cos (born approx. 470-460 BC, died approx. 389-360 BC).

The truth is that we have no defense. The notion of autonomy-*It's my choice when and how I die*-runs contrary to the sovereignty of God. Psalm 139 says that God has numbered our days-He sovereignly determines our lifespan before we are even born: "All the days ordained for me were written in your book before one of them came to be."[40]   Satan would love to tempt a suffering believer to take the easy way out, but Jesus reminds us that he is the enemy of our souls. The thief only comes around "to steal, and *to kill*, and to destroy." Moreover, Satan loves to tempt an unbeliever to end his or her life prematurely, before they can make a decision that would change their eternal destiny by choosing Christ.

A human life, whether an embryo or an eighty year old, is sacred and it must be protected. To discard humans with no thought of moral consequence is damning to your eternal soul. The Lord shines a light on the punishment for those who disregard human life:

"Do not give any of your children to be sacrificed...
do not defile yourself in any of these ways,
because this is how the nations that I am

---

40 Psalm 139:16

going to drive out before you became defiled.
Even the land was defiled; so I punished it for
its sin, and vomited out its inhabitants."

—Leviticus 18:21,24-25

The Word even goes so far as to mandate capital punishment to those that bring harm to an unborn child.

"If men who are fighting hit a pregnant woman and
she gives birth prematurely but there is no serious
injury, the offender must be fined... but if there is
serious injury, you are to take life for life, eye for eye,
tooth for tooth, hand for hand, foot for foot, burn
for burn, wound for wound, bruise for bruise.

—Exodus 21:22-25

While the word abortion is not explicitly used in any text, the concept of killing an unborn child and its consequences could not be clearer.

The debate over physician assisted suicides, passive and active euthanasia, and abortion begs the question of the sanctity of life and elevates human desire over subjection to divine will. It places function ahead of human uniqueness. However, know this. No matter how many there might be who align themselves against God and the sanctity of human life; dismembering an embryo, killing a fetus, and heart stopping injections to the elderly are all indisputably *murder*. It has always been and it always will be. Regardless of what our earthly judges hold, our heavenly Judge will soon have His day in court and everyone will be held accountable for their actions.

4

Attack on Christianity

"Congress shall make no law respecting
an establishment of religion, or prohibiting
the free exercise thereof..." [1]

Freedom from Religion

Unfortunately the principal guilty party in prohibiting
the free exercise of religion, a guaranteed constitutional
right, has been the Supreme Court. However, Congress

[1] The Constitution of the United States of America, *(Establishment Clause and
Free Exercise Clause of the 1st Amendment, ratified December 15, 1791)*

is not without blame in regard to the Supreme Court overruling the expressed will of the people. Under Article III Section 2 of the United States Constitution, the Congress has the power to regulate the appellate jurisdiction of the Federal Courts, yet Congress has rarely been so bold to speak out against the judiciary. Those who hail "separation of church and state" and attempt to forbid anything to enter the public sector whose origins are remotely Christian need to realize that the Constitution guarantees the free exercise of religion... *even* Christianity.

It is no secret that our forefathers fled England to escape abuse of governmental power.[2] The ideal behind our Republic and the concept of federalism, is that most of the control lies with the people and the states; it is not held in a centralized government.[3] The Declaration of Independence shines on the roots of our nation's moral foundations:

We hold these truths to be self evident, that all men are created equal, that they are endowed by their Creator with certain unalienable Rights, that among these are Life, Liberty and the pursuit of Happiness.

---

2 Dr. Norman Geisler & Frank Turek, *Legislating Morality*, 1998 p.18
3 James Madison, Alexander Hamilton, and John Jay, *The Federalist Papers*, Number 39 and 51: First published in 1788.

Dr. Normal Geisler, Dean of the Veritas Graduate School in Charlotte, North Carolina, points out that the "Founding Fathers, in accordance with Moral Law, affirmed their belief in (1) a Creator (God), (2) Creation (that man was created), and (3) God given moral absolutes (that man has God given 'unalienable rights')."[4] So why did we depart from our roots?

The shift from the will of the people to the imposition of the will of the court has been a gradual one—this did not happen overnight. It did not explicitly happen when prayer was thrown out of schools, when abortions were made legal, or when the Ten Commandments were removed from public buildings at the insistence of the ACLU. The seed was planted long before. The problem within our society today is that the majority of our citizens have turned their backs on moral absolutes. There is no right and there is no wrong—everything is relative. Humanism, defined as a "nonreligious philosophy based on liberal human values,"[5] has saturated our society, little by little, and as a result we are racing down the road to complete and total moral annihilation.

---

[4] ibid. p.58
[5] The Oxford Desk Dictionary, 1995: p. 273

Now more than ever people seek freedom *from* religion. After all, if there is no God in heaven to decide what is right and wrong, then it is man's prerogative to determine right and wrong. It is this philosophy that has increasingly eroded our spiritual rights. Man feels there is no superior authority to his own. With man no longer looking to a deity, but rather looking to himself, he is no longer held accountable by the moral code he once knew. If he can ignore God, he can ignore God's laws such as The Ten Commandments and the Bible. Instead he permits himself to do otherwise. Never before has there been such polarization between good and evil in our society and the world at large. We are facing a war against Christianity and a cultural war for the soul of the nation.

Mass murder, genocide, and loss of civil rights are no longer stories reserved for third world countries or history books. We have read of millions being murdered in Nazi concentration camps, yet now we accomplish the same in our abortion mills. We have studied the excess and sexual debauchery of the Roman Empire, yet we have a multibillion dollar pornography industry fueled by lust and debased desire. We condemn Middle Eastern governments for forcing their citizens to only worship one god, yet attack Christians for wanting to worship their God.

In Psalm 2, a prophetic Psalm, David describes a generation where the leaders of the world rise in revolt against both Christians and Jews. We are that generation. The Word says, "Why do the nations conspire and the peoples plot in vain?" "The kings of the earth take their stand and the rulers gather together against the Lord and against his Anointed One." "Let us break their chains," they say, "and throw off their fetters."[6] The focus of this rebellion that David speaks about is God and Christ. The kings of the earth take their stand by "breaking their chains" or the restraints that the Word of God imposes on society. Sadly enough we are succeeding at doing just that. Look at the worldwide movements whose purpose was and is to cast God out of society: Communism, where the state is the god; Atheism, where there is no god; Secular Humanism, where man is God; and New Age, everything and anything is god... except Christianity.

---

6 Psalm 2:1-3

Freedom of religion... as long as you are not a Christian

Nothing that is morally right
can ever be politically wrong.

—Anonymous

Many assume that "separation of church and state" appears somewhere in the Constitution. It does not. The first amendment of the Constitution prohibits the making of laws that respect the establishment of religion and prohibit its free exercise. As a result, our lawmakers have made it impossible for public school children to recite Christian prayer in public schools. However, as was reported in December 2003, a California school in the Byron Union School District is requiring seventh-grade students to "pretend they're Muslims, wear Islamic garb, memorize verses from the Quran, pray to Allah and even to play 'jihad games'."[7] A federal judge upheld that such activities were allowable after outraged Christian parents brought a lawsuit against the school district.[8]

---

[7] "Judicial Jihad," World Net Daily, posted December 13, 2003. www.worldnet-daily.com
[8] *Thomas More Law Center v. Byron Union School District 2003*

While courts are allowing *other* religions to be promoted, Christianity is still being targeted. In May 1995, Samuel B. Kent, U.S. District Judge for the Southern District of Texas, decreed that any student uttering the word "Jesus" at a school graduation would be arrested and incarcerated for six months. His words deserve to be quoted at some length:

> "And make no mistake... the court is going to have a United States Marshall in attendance at the graduation. If any student offends this court, that student will be summarily arrested and will face up to six months incarceration in the Galveston County jail for contempt of court. Anyone who violates these orders is going to wish that he or she had died as a child when this court gets through with it.[9]

Unfortunately this incident is not an isolated one. A teacher at Lynn Lucas Middle School in Houston, Texas shouted, "This is garbage" as she threw two students' Bibles into the trash can. The teacher then took the

---

9 "Exploring the Myth of Church-State Separation" <u>Whistleblower Magazine,</u> posted December 4, 2003

students to the principal's office, called their parents, and threatened to call Child Protective Services because Bibles were not permitted on school property. Additionally, in that same school, those students whose books had the Ten Commandments displayed on the covers were ordered by school officials to throw them out, alleging that the Ten Commandments were "hate speech."[10]

The attacks don't stop there. When a seven year old was asked to a bring a book to her classroom show and tell to share her Christmas traditions her teacher barred her from reading it due to the fact that it mentioned Jesus Christ. The teacher said, "Its religious content made it inappropriate."[11] When the school principal was confronted by the child's parents the principal reiterated that students could, "share books about their Christmas traditions so long as those books were not religious."[12] Another example of this anti-Christian bias occurred in Alabama when a District Court Judge issued an injunction against school prayer. The judge held that prayers were not permitted in any fashion including,

[10] Harvey Rice, "Lawsuit Claims Students Not Allowed to Carry Bibles" *Houston Chronicle* May 23,2000
[11] "School Assignment: Open Discussion of Christmas But Not Allowed to Mention Christ." Boston Globe July 30, 2002, *(posted on www.underreported.com August 2,2002)*
[12] ibid.

"prayers on the school PA system during Veterans Day or times of national crisis."[13] He also went on to categorize students' lunchtime prayers as "disruptive, aggressive, harassing speech by students, even in such a lunch setting, and is not protected."[14]

Another startling example of attack on Christianity took place when Texas Tech biology professor, Michael Dini, refused to write letters of recommendation to medical school for students who would not acknowledge their acceptance of the theory of evolution. Dr. James Brink, the assistant provost, showed support for Professor Dini, citing that students with strong faith and a belief in creationism should not attend public universities.[15]

Regarding higher education, noted history professor George Marsden claims that, "In the most prestigious parts of American academia, religious scholars are given less of a voice than Marxist scholars."[16] Christian Evangelist Chuck Colson had this to say about academic freedom in American universities:

---

[13] Larry Mundinger et al. "Judge Ira Dement Issues New Warning in Alabama Prayer Case," November 17, 1997 www.positiveatheism.com
[14] ibid.
[15] Michael Castellon, "Controversy Arises from Professors Policy" *The University Daily*, October 24, 2002.
[16] "A Truly Multicultural Society" October 2000 (an e-mail exchange between George Marsden and *The Atlantic's* Wen Stephenson, www.theatlantic.com)

We are left with a disturbing paradox.
While higher education is better funded
and more accessible than ever before... it
has nothing left worth teaching... there is
no truth worth pursuing.[17]

These are only a very few examples of how Christianity is being blatantly berated in our society.

Our past presidents have thought education and Christianity go hand in hand. George Washington said, "The future of this nation depends on the Christian training of our youth. It is impossible to govern America without the Bible."[18] Likewise, Abraham Lincoln highlights the importance of education by saying, "The philosophy of the school room in one generation will be the philosophy of government in the next."[19] We must do as the Word says and "train a child in the way he should go, and when he is old he will not turn from it."[20] However, we have not been training our children in the right way—and in the event that we do not, the state will.

---

[17] Charles Colson, *Against the Night: Living in the New Dark Ages.* 1989, p.85
[18] *Halley's Bible Handbook,* Zondervan, 1965, pp.18-19
[19] Revival Insights Vol. IV, No. 10
[20] Proverbs 22:6

The founder of Secular Humanism, Charles F. Potter, wrote:

> Education is the most powerful ally of humanism. What can a Sunday school, meeting for one hour a week, and teaching only a fraction of the children, do to stem the tide of a five-day humanistic teaching?[21]

Many people ignorantly think "secular" means neutral. This is wrong! Secular Humanism is a world-wide religion whose goal is to expel every other faith. As the authors of the Humanist Manifesto delicately state, "We find insufficient evidence for belief in the existence of a supernatural; it is either meaningless or irrelevant to the question of survival and fulfillment of the human race."[22] Secular Humanism is a non-neutral and religious faith. It is its own religion with its own precepts. The Christian religion is being openly condemned and its symbols are considered illegal. Meanwhile secular humanism is preached and propagated from most public schools and universities.

---

[21] Charles Francis Potter, *Humanism: A New Religion*, 1930. p. 128
[22] Paul Kurtz & Edwin H. Wilson, *Humanist Manifesto II* 1973

A huge double standard presents itself. For instance, look to the hypocrisy of the Supreme Court. They open each session with the words, "God save the United States and this honorable court," and chaplains in both houses of Congress open the days with invocations. One recent prayer from Congress included, "Blessed is the nation whose God is the Lord."[23] The Court made Alabama Chief Justice Roy Moore remove the monument of the Ten Commandments that was in front of the Courthouse; however a sculpture of Moses and the Ten Commandments adorns the top of the United States Supreme Court building. The sculpture, entitled "Justice the Guardian of Liberty" by Herman McNeil, is the most noticeable icon in the entire façade; ironically the Chief Justice's offices are directly behind this portico.[24] A current prayer in the House reads, "You, Lord, will lead, guide, and direct them in their affairs." The same day the Senate prayed, "Fill our God-shaped void with Your presence and bid our striving to cease."[25] Is this not the same group that prohibits the religious freedoms of their constituents while openly practicing Christianity themselves? Where does our government stand, and why are we allowing this to happen?

---

[23] Siobhan McDonough, "Religion embedded in U.S. society, government, courts" *The Washington Times*, August 24, 2003
[24]"Moses Image Adorns U.S. Supreme Court Building", posted August 20, 2003 by www.freerepublic.com
[25] ibid.

The Diluted Constitution

"Do not let anyone claim to be a true American if they ever attempt to remove religion from politics".

—George Washington

We can sit and point our finger at the Courts and Congress; however, at the end of the day it is the constituents who are allowing these atrocities against the free exercise of Christianity to be perpetuated. We have stayed mum while pundits and politicians have thrown convoluted reasons as to why a godless society is a better one; yet when faced with the realities of what a godless society entails we choose to get upset. We must stop accepting their excuses and mandate a change—we must demand freedom of religion for Christians.

Too many times we have heard activist judges and leaders alike who add and subtract from the Constitution as if it were a math problem. How much clearer can the following words be? "Congress shall make no law respecting an establishment of religion, or prohibit the free exercise thereof." Yet from that sentence our lawmakers have deduced that God must be ushered out of society. The Constitution has been manipulated to endorse whatever the courts feel is necessary.

Consider the following comparison: when the Supreme Court was asked to rule on constitutionality of the right to abortion, it held that abortions were constitutionally permissible because the right to privacy "is broad enough to encompass a woman's decision whether or not to terminate her pregnancy."[26] Of course there is no "right to privacy" mentioned in the Constitution. The Court held that this right was found in the "penumbras" or shadows of the document.[27] A right of privacy may or may not be constitutionally acceptable, and the right may or may not have any bearing on the abortion issue—but it has become all too typical for an activist court to work hard to search the "shadows" of the Constitution to discover a right to kill the unborn, yet at the same time restrict freedoms in the face of the explicit injunction to do otherwise.

Lawmakers redundantly resound that it is impossible to know what the framers intended when they wrote the

Constitution. While this may be true, the framers did leave some guidelines in regard to constitutional interpretation. In a letter to William Johnson, Thomas Jefferson wrote:

> On every question of construction (of the Constitution) let us carry ourselves back to the time when the Constitution was adopted, recollect the spirit manifested in the debates, and instead of trying what meaning may be squeezed out of the text, or invented against it, conform to the probable one in which it was passed.[28]

Instead of conforming to the probable meaning of the Constitution, our society continually abuses the freedoms the document was meant to protect. It has already been established that despite the fact that the 1st Amendment is supposed to enable our freedom to worship, our laws have prohibited it. Yet in the meantime all other deviant behaviors–such as burning American flags, torching draft cards, gratuitous use of profanity in public arenas, and glorification of violence— are all acceptable under the scope of freedoms

[28] Thomas Jefferson, letter to William Johnson, June 12, 1823, *The Complete Jefferson*, p. 322

guaranteed by the 1st Amendment. Allowing this to continue is only going to further cripple the moral foundation of our nation; freedom without "reasonable and responsible limits destroys individual lives and ultimately destroys the fabric of a civilized society."[29]

Some may say that our government cannot legislate morality, but it does so everyday. Keeping God out of the picture is not going to stop that from taking place. Does our society not prohibit rape? Is murder not also illegal? What about theft? Our government thinks that it is morally wrong to commit these offenses, thus the government legislates against them.[30] Ironically enough God also "legislates" against these offenses in His Ten Commandments. What is God's reaction to man's efforts to kick Him out? The Word tells us, "The kings of the earth take their stand and the rulers gather together against the Lord and against His Anointed One... the One enthroned in heaven laughs; the Lord scoffs at them."[31] No matter how hard lawmakers try to keep morality and religion out of politics, they will always fail to do so.

If it is inevitable that government legislate morality—

---

[29] ibid. Geisler & Turek p. 16
[30] ibid. p.24
[31] Proverbs 2:2,4

that some sort of religious perspective lies at the foundation of our efforts in this republican form of government—then why should we cede the ground to those who hate Christianity? In fact, it could be argued, that "we the people" are the true sovereigns in a republican form of government, and every curse leveled by God against corrupt and perverted regimes in the past will be leveled on us if we do not claim the sovereignty that is rightfully ours!

5

Making an Impact

Let each citizen remember at the moment
he is offering his vote that he is not making a
present or a compliment to please an
individual—or at least that he ought not so to
do; but that he is executing one of the most
solemn trusts in human society for which he is
accountable to God and his country.

—Samuel Adams[1]

The battle lines are now drawn. We must now prepare
ourselves to make an impact on our society and be a

---

[1] Samuel Adams, *The Writings of Samuel Adams*, Harry Alonzo Cushing, editor (New
York: G.P. Putnam's Sons, 1907), Vol. IV, p. 256, in the *Boston Gazette* on April 16, 1781.

good witness to those around us. Too many times in our society Christians are being portrayed to be extremely judgmental, with nothing to offer society but criticism and negative attitudes. "Christianity is a great idea. Too bad no one has tried it." These words, spoken by a famous British playwright and cynic, Oscar Wilde, reflect an all too familiar stereotype regarding Christianity. Bertrand Russell, the most famous atheist in the beginning of the twentieth century, said that, "The reason I am not a Christian is because I know too many Christians." Words like these are a tragic indictment of the followers of Jesus Christ; sadly enough in many cases they are true. Petty, judgmental, legalistic, and hypocritical people fill the pews of many of today's churches. It is those with scathing attitudes and actions that solicit such negative comments from people like Wilde, Russell and a large portion of society.

This cliché can no longer be perpetuated. We must accurately convey to society that, while we are a political force to be reckoned with, we are also a caring people that only want the best for our collective futures and the future of our children and grandchildren. A Christian's failure to "preach the gospel" with actions and deeds can cause people to repel from God and the gospel. If Christians are fueled by malice, greed, and judgment, the world will not receive what we have to say; rather they will be condemned for our hypocrisy.

Christians will not be able to change anything unless we change ourselves. We must demonstrate to society that we have something they want, something they are missing. We must convey to the world that Christianity is not something to be endured, but something to be treasured. Instead of legalism, we must offer them life; instead of liturgy, we must offer them liberty; and instead of loathing, we must offer them love. With the current moral climate in the world today, people should be standing in line to get into church. We need to give them a reason to do so. We must change our lives to reflect Christ in us, let our light shine, and change the world.

This is our challenge, a challenge for which we will be accountable to the Lord Jesus Christ, whom we serve. Will we have brought improvement to the world; healing to mankind or will we allow the darkness to envelop us and create more darkness in the process? Our Creator gives us a choice. If not now, when? If not us, then who?

Political Involvement

*"Nothing is so fatal to religion as indifference
which is, at least, half infidelity"*
—**Edmund Burke**

Burke claims that "indifference" is fatal to religion; the same can be said of the political process. To be apathetic towards the laws that control your life and the lives of your children is to be an unfaithful American. We need to do more than cast our vote. We need to set the terms of debate and let our voices be heard. We must start in our own communities and let our influence at home be heard all the way to the White House.

Usually when you ask most people to name an elective office, virtually everyone will say president, vice-president, senator, governor, or other high-profile offices. People forget that there are precinct elections after every primary election, and that the results of these precinct caucuses shape the agenda of the state party conventions later in that year. At the precinct meeting, which is held after the polls close at the same location where you voted, your neighbors will elect delegates to the county or district convention and will vote on resolutions to be proposed for the party platform.

This process is repeated at the county or district level, where delegates to the state convention are elected and recommendations for the party platform are debated and voted upon. At the state convention, delegates to the national convention are elected, and at the national convention the final version of the party platform is adopted. It's possible for a resolution started by average citizens at a precinct meeting to travel all the way to the national party convention where the party's presidential nominee is selected.

Political parties are like any other organization. Organizational loyalty, frequency of participation in party events, and longevity of association all count for influence in a political party. One of the unique aspects of our American political structure—which for all its weakness is hailed as the best in the world—is that plain, average persons are not only allowed to vote, but also to have a larger impact in the political process.

Political involvement goes further than casting a vote. Edmund Burke, political philosopher and statesman, once said, "It is a general popular error to suppose the loudest complainers for the public to be the most anxious for its welfare." We must do more than stand on our soapbox and complain. We will not be acknowledged for the problems we recognize, but for the problems we help solve.

We can all get involved in the political process by volunteering in local campaigns, making financial contributions to a worthy candidate, fundraising, or supporting voter registration drives. Involvement can be taken even further by trying to influence opinion in public forums by writing letters to the editor of newspapers, calling into radio talk shows to voice our informed opinion, and bring to the surface issues that are important to sustain traditional values in America. We can even run for precinct or county offices. Somebody has to fill the lower offices in our system, so why not us?

Elective offices in our nation periodically open up for the general population to once again vote for candidates they believe will best represent their value systems as they fulfill the governmental powers accorded the office. Someone has to run—someone will—and someone will be elected. Why can't that someone be a person who loves Jesus Christ and who considers their governmental position to be a sacred trust? Our nation is a sum of its parts; it can only be as good as the individuals who live in it and lead it. We are those individuals; what are we doing to make our nation be the best it can be? If not us... then who? If not now... when?

"The only thing necessary for the triumph of evil is for good men to do nothing.

—Edmund Burke

Casting Your Vote

In the Sermon on the Mount, Jesus not only told His followers that they were the light of the world; He also said they were the salt of the earth.[2] Salt is meant to season and to preserve. It is important for us to be the "salt" that seasons our communities with moral virtue as prescribed in the Word of God. It is equally important to take seriously the preservation function of "salt" by translating the truth into votes.

First we must understand that, as Bible-believing

---

2 Matthew 5:13

Christians, our views and our political priorities will always be unpopular. Most people are not going to agree with us on everything. The Lord reminds us that the way to heaven is through a "narrow gate" and "there are few who find it."[3] Believers are often going to be outnumbered, and if we are to prevail we must stick together and each do our part to stand for righteousness. Because we are the minority, it is doubly important that each Christian register to vote and get involved in the political process. Above all, it is critical that we not just register to vote but that we go the polls and cast our vote. The only tangible way Jesus Christ is going to have a "voice" in each election is for each follower to express that voice by means of prayerfully casting a ballot on the issues.

While the decision to change can be made in the space of a moment of prayer, changing governmental structures and the way people vote can take years. Here at the cusp of change in an election year, we have two major political parties in America. One is the home where most advocate homosexuality, abortion, maximum taxation, unlimited handouts, and little freedom from government control. The other major party is the home of social conservatives who for the

---

3 Matthew 7:13-14

most part believe in the sanctity of life, hard work, clean moral living, limited government interference, minimum taxation, and a return to Bible-based societal values. We as Christians must choose our party and our candidates based on our convictions dictated in the Word of God.

The way to keep a political party accountable to their constituents is to go to the ballot box. Because so many do not cast their vote on Election Day, in many cases Americans end up being governed by a relatively small percentage of the population. During a 2000 primary campaign in Texas it was estimated that a mere three percent of registered voters would determine the result for the other 97 percent of the people that didn't bother to vote. If people of righteousness would see to it that there was a candidate running in each election who shared our Godly values, and if all Christians voted for that person, then America would have an opportunity to climb out of the moral decline we have experienced in the last several decades.

God's Candidate for America

It is our responsibility to stand up and speak out for the

traditional values that made America the greatest nation in the world. Qualified Christians should stand for elective office; we should seek out and serve as appointed officials whenever possible; we should see to it that our children receive a higher education so that they will be qualified to lead the next generation.

In a nation of 270 million people, there is no reason to tolerate unrighteousness in our governmental offices. With only 535 seats in Congress, one president, one vice-president, and fifty governors, why should we ever settle for less than what is required by God Himself. "Righteousness exalts a nation but sin is a reproach to any people..." The apostle Paul wrote to the Corinthian believers that all Christians are "ambassadors of Christ."[4] An ambassador is an official representative of a specific government. We must be Christ's ambassadors in the voting booth, and there is no time like the present to start. If we want to be the salt of the earth, if we want to let our light shine, if we want to make a difference in this nation, we must not be afraid to take a stand and legislate morality that will help shape society for the better. If we do not, someone else will, and they will control your fate. We must choose God's candidate for America.

4[4] 2 Corinthians 5:20

In 1832 Noah Webster spoke on the importance of voting. Almost prophetically he has painted the face of American voters and what their apathy has meant to our political system. He states:

"When you become entitled to exercise the right of voting for public officers, let it be impressed upon your mind that God commands you to choose for rulers, 'just men who will rule in the fear of God.' The preservation of government depends on the faithful discharge of this duty; if the citizens neglect their duty and place unprincipled men in office, the government will soon be corrupted; laws will be made, not for the public good so much as for selfish or local purposes; corrupt or incompetent men will be appointed to execute the laws; and the rights of the citizens will be violated or disregarded. If a republican government fails to secure public prosperity and happiness, it must be because the citizens neglect the divine commands, and elect bad men to administer the laws."[5]

5 posted on Chuck Colson's commentary, "A Sacred Duty: Why Christians Must Vote" May 14, 2004 (www.townhall.com)

We must unite and endeavor to preserve our government. We must understand exactly what is at stake when we step into a voting booth. We will only have as much freedom as we are willing to fight for. We must unite and we must fight, because our future depends on it. The Lord says in the book of Jeremiah 9:23:

> *"Let not the wise man glory in his wisdom, let not the rich man glory in his wealth, but he who wishes to glory, let him glory in this... that he understands and knows Me, for I am the Lord who exercises loving-kindness, justice and righteousness in the earth, for it is in these things that I delight, saith the Lord."*

The Lord delights in justice and righteousness. He gives us the ability to choose for righteousness through our right to vote. We must all exercise our God-given right for the sake of our country and the future of our children.

Guidelines for Church and Clergy

There has been much confusion as to what a church and Pastor can and can't do. The following are guidelines intended to direct civic leaders to do what is legal under the law. These guidelines were taken and influenced by materials distributed through Concerned Women for America.

1. **A church can educate its members on issues that affect the moral condition of the country, the education of our children, and the involvement of its members in the political process.**

A church can educate the congregation by preaching from the pulpit, teaching in Sunday school classes, sponsoring seminars on topics such as Bible positions on political issues, and providing literature for distribution of educational materials.

Another way to educate its members is by hosting or conducting a nonpartisan candidate forum in which candidates debate or discuss their views on relevant issues of interest to the general public. All candidates for a particular office in question should be invited to participate to avoid bias for or against any particular candidate or party.

2. **A church can participate in "legislative activity" as long as it does not exceed 5% of the overall activity of the church's programs. Anything**

over 5% has either been questioned or held unacceptable under the section 501(c) 3 of the Internal Revenue Code.

"Legislative activity" is defined as any conduct intended to influence legislation—bills before the U.S. Congress and state legislatures, measures before city councils, initiatives and referendums. These cover actions such as contacting legislators about legislation, urging church members and others to communicate with legislators about legislation, and circulating petitions related to specific legislation.

3. **A church can engage in voter registration and voter education projects such as "get-out-the vote" drives. The church may spend money to pay registration organizers or to mail out registration forms. You may contact your local voter registration office for forms and procedures.**

The voter registration drive must be nonpartisan, not showing any bias for or against a candidate or political party. No display of campaign materials on specific issues that will create a bias for or against a certain candidate, or urge voters to register for a particular party should be present.

4. **A church may not endorse or oppose a candidate for public office.** Additionally, when a Pastor is speaking on behalf of his church, he cannot endorse or oppose a candidate for public office.

5. **A pastor of a church may, as an individual, personally endorse or oppose a candidate. This endorsement should occur on personal time and not from his pulpit to prevent the endorsement from being attributed to the church.**

Additionally, if a pastor lends his name to a candidate for political advertisements or devotes personal time to a candidate's campaign, his title may be listed with his name for the purpose of identification. The fact that a church employs the pastor does not negate his constitutional rights of free speech and political expression.

6. **Candidates may be introduced to a congregation in the course of a service. In addition, candidates may be allowed to preach,**

teach, and read scriptures on the same basis as other church members or participants. However, a candidate should not be allowed to deliver political speeches to gain support or raise funds for his campaign.

7. A church may not contribute money or raise funds for a political party or a candidate for public office. If the church is incorporated the Federal Election Campaign Act prohibits any corporation from making contributions or expenditures in connection with a federal campaign.

8. Candidates should not be allowed to use church facilities or property for political purposes because it may be viewed equivalent to a contribution.

9. A church may not loan its membership or mailing list to a candidate or political committee for use in an election campaign.

10. A church may distribute voter guides educating their members on the voting records of all candidates running for office. A voter

guide should report the views of all candidates by publishing their public records or publishing their responses to unbiased, nonpartisan questionnaires.

Our nation and our government are in desperate need of the "salt and light" that only the Church, her pastors, and her people can provide. By understanding and creatively using the lawful means at our disposal, we can make a difference!

(This information is intended to a general discussion and should not be interpreted as a legal devise. Churches or pastors needing advice on a particular circumstance should ask the counsel of their own legal or tax advisors.)

Other Informational Resources

Federal Election Commission
Register to Vote Online at: www.fec.gov

Family Research Council (FRC)
www.frc.org
This is an invaluable source of statistics and information on family policy issues.

Contact your Senator
www.senate.gov
Starting petitions in on issues in your church and neighborhoods makes a huge impact.

Contact your Congressman
www.house.gov

Tools for Letter Writing and Voting Records
www.trimonline.com
Know where your representatives stand.

Traditional Values
www.traditonalvalues.org
A constant source of information, polls, studies and tools for Conservative voters.